Hello, Family Members,

Learning to read is one of the most im[illegible] of early childhood. **Hello Reader!** bo[illegible] children become skilled readers who like to read. Beginning readers learn to read by remembering frequently used words like "the," "is," and "and"; by using phonics skills to decode new words; and by interpreting picture and text clues. These books provide both the stories children enjoy and the structure they need to read fluently and independently. Here are suggestions for helping your child *before*, *during*, and *after* reading:

Before

- Look at the cover and pictures and have your child predict what the story is about.
- Read the story to your child.
- Encourage your child to chime in with familiar words and phrases.
- Echo read with your child by reading a line first and having your child read it after you do.

During

- Have your child think about a word he or she does not recognize right away. Provide hints such as "Let's see if we know the sounds" and "Have we read other words like this one?"
- Encourage your child to use phonics skills to sound out new words.
- Provide the word for your child when more assistance is needed so that he or she does not struggle and the experience of reading with you is a positive one.
- Encourage your child to have fun by reading with a lot of expression . . . like an actor!

After

- Have your child keep lists of interesting and favorite words.
- Encourage your child to read the books over and over again. Have him or her read to brothers, sisters, grandparents, and even teddy bears. Repeated readings develop confidence in young readers.
- Talk about the stories. Ask and answer questions. Share ideas about the funniest and most interesting characters and events in the stories.

I do hope that you and your child enjoy this book.

—Francie Alexander
Reading Specialist,
Scholastic's Instructional Publishing Group

To Kathy Lande,
librarian *par excellence*
—K.M.

To Kim Kurki
—M.S.

Library of Congress Cataloging-in-Publication Data available.
ISBN 0-590-51222-6

10 9 8 7 6 5 4 3 0/0 01 02 03

Printed in the U.S.A. 24
First printing, September 1998

by Kate McMullan
Illustrated by Mavis Smith

Hello Reader! — Level 3

SCHOLASTIC INC.

New York Toronto London Auckland Sydney

Count Fluffula

It was Halloween.
Everyone in Ms. Day's class
wore a costume to school.
Everyone except Fluffy.

“Ms. Day!” said Maxwell.
“Fluffy needs a costume!”
Right, thought Fluffy.
I need a scary costume.
I am one scary pig!

"I know!" said Jasmine.

"Fluffy can be a pirate!"

Yo ho ho! thought Peg Leg Fluffy.

I sail the seven seas!

Don't mess with me

or I will make you walk the plank!

"Fluffy could be a mummy," said Wade.

I am coming out of my tomb,

thought King Fluffy.

Shake with fear when you see me!

"I have it," said Maxwell.
"Fluffy can be an alien space pig!"
I am from Mars!
thought Space Pig Fluffy.
Take me to your leader!

“Think quickly, class,” said Ms. Day.
“The big Halloween parade
is about to begin.”

“We could tape a string tail
to Fluffy’s back end,” said Maxwell.
“Then Fluffy could be a rat.”
A rat? thought Fluffy. **Never!**
“I have a better idea,” said Emma.
ANY idea is better than a rat!
thought Fluffy.

"Fluffy can be a baby," said Emma.

Who, me? thought Fluffy.

"Yes!" said Jasmine.

"I will make a little diaper for him."

Oh, no, thought Fluffy.

Nobody is putting a diaper on ME!

Fluffy dashed over to his food bowl.
He dove under a big lettuce leaf
and hid.

"Ms. Day?" said Wade.

"Can the person with the scariest costume lead the parade?"

"All right," said Ms. Day.

Fluffy stayed under the lettuce leaf.

He did not want anyone to find him.

He felt hungry.

He wished he had not eaten both his carrots.

But he had.

Only two dried-up carrot tips were left.

Fluffy started to eat them.

“Hey!” Maxwell said suddenly.
“I don’t see Fluffy!”
“Fluffy!” called Jasmine. “Where are you?”
Fluffy forgot that he was hiding.
He sat up.

“Look, Ms. Day!” said Jasmine.
“Fluffy has on a vampire costume!”
“He’s scary,” said Wade.
“Let’s have Fluffy lead the parade.”
“You mean,” said Emma, “Count Fluffula!”

So Count Fluffula
led the big Halloween parade.
I told you, thought Count Fluffula.
I am one scary pig.

Fluffy and the Pumpkin of Doom

Mr. Lee's class invited Ms. Day's class to their spook house.

"You can come, too," Wade told Fluffy. "Just don't get scared."

Me? thought Fluffy. **I am never scared.**

Wade carried Fluffy to Mr. Lee's classroom.

There was a sign on the door. It said:

Mr. Lee's classroom was very dark.

"Are you scared?" Wade asked Fluffy.

Not me, thought Fluffy.

I am never scared.

Wade took Fluffy
into the spook house.
Jared jumped out at them.
He had hair on his face.
He had hair on his hands.
Jared smiled. His teeth were pointed.

"Oooowwwww!" Jared howled.
"I am Wolf Boy!"
I'm not scared, thought Fluffy.
But get me out of here!

"Cool fangs," said Wade.
"I have an extra pair,"
Wolf Boy told Wade.
"Here. Try them on."

Wade put Fluffy down.
He tried on the fangs.
"You look great!" Wolf Boy said.
"Let's go show Ms. Day."
Wade ran off with Wolf Boy.
Hey! thought Fluffy. **Wait for me!**
But Wade did not wait.
Soon Fluffy could not see him anymore.

I am in a spook house,
thought Fluffy.
It is a very scary place.
It is a good thing I am never scared.
Fluffy began walking.
He hoped he was walking
out of the spook house.
I am never scared, thought Fluffy.
Never, never, never. Not me.

Fluffy walked around a corner.
Suddenly a little ghost
jumped out at him.
Boo! yelled the ghost.
Aaaahhhhhhh! yelled Fluffy.
He jumped up in the air.

"Wow!" said Lina from Mr. Lee's class.

"You scared him!"

Lina pulled a scarf off the ghost.

Fluffy gasped.

The ghost was Kiss!

Ha, ha! Kiss laughed.

You should have seen

the silly look on your face!

You looked so scared!

Fluffy did not know what to say,
so he turned and ran.
He ran out of the spook house.
He saw a jack-o'-lantern on the floor.
Fluffy jumped into it.
He tried to catch his breath.

Fluffy looked through
the jack-o'-lantern's mouth.
He saw Kiss.
She was coming out of the spook house.
She was still laughing.
I will show her, thought Fluffy.

Fluffy waited.

Kiss came close to the jack-o'-lantern.

STOP! yelled Fluffy.

Kiss stopped.

She looked around.

Uh...who said that? she asked.

ME! yelled Fluffy.

THE PUMPKIN OF DOOM!

Yikes! said Kiss.

Please do not hurt me,

Mr. Pumpkin of Doom!

Fluffy gave a terrible growl.

I AM GOING TO EAT YOU UP!

Aaaahhhhhhh! screamed Kiss.
She jumped up in the air.
She kept screaming as she ran away.
Now THAT is scared, thought Fluffy.

Wade found Fluffy
inside the jack-o'-lantern.
He picked Fluffy up
and took him back to Ms. Day's room.
"Were you scared?" Wade asked.
Not me, thought Fluffy.
I am never scared.

Fluffy and the Monster Eyeballs

On Halloween night, Wade took Fluffy
to Jasmine's house for a Halloween party.
Jasmine's big brother Jake
stood at the door.
He wore a white coat and big glasses.

“I am Dr. Frankenstein!” Jake said.
“I am making a monster.
Go into my monster lab.
See my monster parts.
They will make you scream!”
“Cool!” said Wade.
Uh..., thought Fluffy.
I just remembered something.
I don’t like to scream.

Wade took Fluffy inside.
Lots of kids were there.
They all went into the monster lab.
I just remembered something,
thought Fluffy.
I don't like monsters.

Jasmine sat at a table inside the lab.
She was dressed as a mad scientist.
Wade put Fluffy down on the table.

Jasmine held up a glass.

It was full of something red.

“This is monster blood!” Jasmine said.

“Cool!” said all the kids.

Gross! thought Fluffy.

I don’t like monster blood!

Next Jasmine held out a bowl
of stringy white mush.
"This is the monster brain," said Jasmine.
"Who wants to touch the monster brain?"
No way! thought Fluffy.
But all the kids stuck their hands
into the bowl.

"Ewww!" they all screamed.
"This is one slimy brain!" said Wade.
I just remembered something,
thought Fluffy.
I don't like monster brains.

Jasmine held out her hand.

“These are the monster eyeballs,”

she said.

“Who wants to touch the monster eyeballs?”

Why would ANYBODY want to?

thought Fluffy.

All the kids wanted to.

“Squishy eyeballs!” said Wade.

I am going to lose my supper!

thought Fluffy.

“Time for the costume contest!”
called Jake.
Jasmine and Wade and all the kids
ran out of the lab.
Wade left Fluffy on the table.
Fluffy sniffed at the monster eyeballs.
His own eyeballs grew very big.
The monster eyeballs smelled
like something he had smelled before.
He sniffed again.
The monster eyeballs smelled like grapes!

A few minutes later,
Wade ran back in to get Fluffy.
"Sorry, Fluffy," he said.
"I forgot about you."
No problem, thought Fluffy.

EYEBALLS
BLOOD

At the end of the party,
all the kids wanted to go back
into the monster lab again.
"Jake!" called Jasmine.
"The monster eyeballs are gone.
I can't find them anywhere."
"Too bad," said Jake.
"I thought the eyeballs
were the best things in the monster lab."

Right, thought Fluffy.
They were delicious!